MW00775188

HECTOR'S
PLACE TO BELONG

THREE STORIES THROUGH THANKSGIVING,
CHRISTMAS, AND EASTER

PATTY JACKSON

Copyright © 2022 Patty Jackson.

All rights reserved. No part of this book may be used or reproduced by
any means, graphic, electronic, or mechanical, including photocopying,
recording, taping or by any information storage retrieval system
without the written permission of the author except in the case of
brief quotations embodied in critical articles and reviews.

This is a work of fiction. All of the characters, names, incidents,
organizations, and dialogue in this novel are either the products
of the author's imagination or are used fictitiously.

LifeRich Publishing is a registered trademark of
The Reader's Digest Association, Inc.

LifeRich Publishing books may be ordered through booksellers or by contacting:

LifeRich Publishing
1663 Liberty Drive
Bloomington, IN 47403
www.liferichpublishing.com
844-686-9607

Because of the dynamic nature of the Internet, any web addresses or
links contained in this book may have changed since publication and
may no longer be valid. The views expressed in this work are solely those
of the author and do not necessarily reflect the views of the publisher,
and the publisher hereby disclaims any responsibility for them.

Any people depicted in stock imagery provided by Getty Images are
models, and such images are being used for illustrative purposes only.
Certain stock imagery © Getty Images.

ISBN: 978-1-4897-4352-7 (sc)
ISBN: 978-1-4897-4351-0 (hc)
ISBN: 978-1-4897-4353-4 (e)

Library of Congress Control Number: 2022915424

Print information available on the last page.

LifeRich Publishing rev. date: 10/19/2022

To my family and husband:
I am blessed to call you friends.

"Not one sparrow can fall to the ground without
your Father knowing it."
Matthew 10:29 NLT

This story began many years ago and I didn't even realize it. I gave my younger brother two mice for Christmas. One mouse insisted on leaving the cage time and time again. Years late in a Worship and the Arts class I had the privilege of a special young woman as a writing partner. Our assignment was to write one page about a person, a place, and an experience from our own childhood. My partner had been homeless for a time and in temporary care of a jealous relative; sharpened fingernails and deep scratching were part of her experience.

Our writing task was to create a fairy tale from the shared information. I cast her as a mouse. "You got me right," she told me. *Hector's Place to Belong* grew out of her story. This steadfast warrior (one meaning of Hector) went on to become a professor in a well-known Bible college.

Miss Annie, a dear aunt, remembered for her kind and creative ways, is an important part of this story. Maya, Dominic, Lyla, Samuel, Olivia, Jackson, Josie, Juniper, Carter, and Luella are my grandchildren.

Stars, a joy of mine, and my grandson's favorite song, "Twinkle, Twinkle, Little Star," are also important. And so, it begins …

STORY 1

A TIME OF THANKS

New Beginnings for Hector

CHAPTER 1

Hector was an almost ordinary field mouse with a rough brown coat, two bright eyes, a friendly face, and a sturdy tail long enough to wrap around his feet. He looked like the rest of his family except for his ears. They all had very small ears tucked against their heads, but Hector's ears were a bit larger and not quite so flat.

And so it happened that one day when he was deep in a blackberry bush and nibbling away, one of his ears caught on a thorn. As he backed away, the end of his ear tore into two parts. It hurt and now looked very strange and not mouse-like at all.

But Mama, who knew things he did not, told him, "Hector, I like your special ear. I don't know any other mouse with a heart-shaped ear. Hearts say 'I love you.' Maybe your ear will help you hear that." And then she whispered in that ear, "I love you very much, Hector."

Hector loved his life on the farm. He played happy games of chase in the corn fields with his large family. Sometimes he traveled into the barn, boldly nibbling grain from under the horse's nose and the chickens' beaks.

His favorite part of the day was after supper. His family

1

gathered at the door of their home to talk together and to watch the sky for the first twinkle of starlight. "Was there anything good about today?" Mama would ask. Someone might talk about the fun game of chase, or all the corn to eat, or the new baby chicks in the barn. They always thanked God for the good gifts of the day and for each other. They closed with a song that Papa had written:

Twinkle, Twinkle little star,

Thank you, God for who you are.

You made things great. You made things small.

You love things great. You love things small.

Twinkle, Twinkle little star,

Thank you, God for who you are."

Then everyone squeezed through the door to flop on top of each other and stay warm while they slept. It was a good way to end a day. It was a very nice life.

CHAPTER 2

Today was "picking day" on the farm. There were lots of people twisting off fresh ears of corn from each plant. Bags of corn were lined up by the barn. The fields were busy and noisy! "Too busy and noisy for me," Hector thought. He made his way to one of the bags and crawled in, "Ah, all quiet and safe in here."

He was busy gnawing on a tender end of an ear of corn when he heard a rough voice, "Come on. Let's move these bags." His bag closed into darkness as it was quickly tied shut and swung through the air. The shifting weight of heavy corn squeezed him hard as the bag was plunked into the back of the truck. Hector turned this way and that until he finally spotted a bit of light and struggled toward it. He climbed out the hole to the top of the bag as the truck bumped along and turned onto a smooth, loud, busy, and smelly road. He watched the only life he had ever known fade away.

"Goodbye family. Goodbye Papa. Goodbye Mama," he called. "I will miss you so."

"Goodbye family."

He dragged himself carefully from the bag, out of the wind, and into a quiet corner. The long ride ended with a sudden stop. He could hear the driver walking toward his hiding place. The back of the truck opened, and the man grabbed one of the bags of corn and turned to hand it to another man.

"How far you going?" the other man asked.

"Just down the road. I'm headed to a local farmer's market. I'm sure this fresh corn will sell quickly."

"Yes, I'm sure too," the other man said. "People like fresh corn."

"And I'm sure I should get off this truck," Hector told himself. And without thinking further, he took a flying leap off the back of the truck before it was closed again. He landed hard with a bone-shaking smack on a cold surface.

As Hector lay breathless and very still, he listened to the truck drive away.

CHAPTER 3

The sun was gone, and darkness was coming. It was chillier by the moment. "If I don't move, I won't be able to," Hector told himself. Slowly he pushed to the edge of the walkway. In the distance he could make out blocks of light, spilling from a building. "Maybe it's a barn. Maybe it will be warm and there will be food inside." Hector scooted as best he could along a dirt path toward the light. It wasn't a door to a barn, but big windows close to a porch. Hector climbed to the corner of the window and peeked in.

People inside were happy and helping themselves to plates of food from a long table. "Oh, please drop a little food," squeaked Hector. He thought of his dashes through the barn. "I'll run in and grab a few bites. I won't bother anyone." He hopefully looked towards the door, but no one was going in or out. He looked for a little hole around the edge of the window, but there was none. He tried gnawing on the window frame, but his teeth would not sink into the hard edging. Hector peered in the window for a long time, hoping someone might notice a cold mouse outside looking very hungry.

But, of course, no one did.

Once the platters of food were cleared, Hector knew it was

time to give up. Never in his life had he felt this hungry, cold, and sad. He dropped into a little heap, trying to stay warm, and wondered what to do.

The Twinkle song suddenly came to mind. "It's that time of night. I can sing our song!" He ran from the window to where he could see just one light in the sky. He looked at it and thought of his family missing him he was sure, and singing. Hector sang as best he could with his tired voice. The sound was a very thin, "Squeak, squeak, squeak." But he knew what he was singing.

"Twinkle, twinkle little star.

Thank you, God, for who you are.

You made things great. You made things small.

You love things great. You love things small ..."

Hector stopped singing, mostly because he did not feel loved at all. "Oh, Great God, do you really love me? I am cold and hungry. I am lonely and sad. It's so hard to feel loved right now!"

Nothing changed right away. No one came out of the house to feed a hungry mouse. No field suddenly appeared. He didn't suddenly feel full.

But he did have an idea. "I will go exploring. That's what I can do."

"Goodbye, star," Hector said as he set off. He stayed close to the house and rounded the corner. And then he stopped. His special ear picked up tiny mousey laughs that sounded very much like his own family.

"A place to belong?" He left the house and followed the squeaky chatter across cold and prickly grass to a burrow under a tree root. Yes, a family of mice were eating an apple with sounds of delight. Hector watched from the doorway—not knowing what to do. All got quiet.

"Who's there?" called the biggest mouse.

"It's, it's, it's me," Hector stammered. "It's Hector, a mouse like you. I'm lost. I miss my mommy and daddy, and I'm, I'm …" Hector would have said, "hungry," but by then he was sniffling so hard he could only give the tiniest of squeaks.

Mama Mouse hurried right over and, taking Hector by the hand, said, "Come in Hector. There is plenty here for you."

Over dinner, Hector found out that this family was the Murphy's. There was Mama Murphy, Papa Murphy, Ruby, Tiffany, George, and Bernard. It was very warm in here, and he gratefully ate with them. Then Mama Murphy said, "You may curl up here, Hector."

Hector pressed into a tiny corner and didn't think too much of Bernard's words, "It's crowded in here, Mama." To Hector, that was a good thing; they were all warm.

CHAPTER 4

The next day, the Murphy children introduced Hector to the "the yard." There were fallen apples to eat and - wonder of wonder - trash bins!

"This trash bin has a secret," Ruby said. She pushed through a broken hole near the bottom, and Hector followed. Inside was a big lumpy black bag. "Now," Ruby said, "we'll climb to the top and take a bite out of the bag. But don't swallow it. Then we'll go through the hole. There's lots of food inside!"

"A bag!" He was so excited at the thought of what might be inside! He had come from being inside a bag of fresh corn! Would it be corn again? Maybe it would be grains and oats and good food like the bags in the barn! Hector did as he was told and gnawed away near the top of the black bag. But as the hole opened, Hector had to admit it did not smell like the farm at all. "Oh well," Hector thought. "Things are new here." He squeezed through the hole and took a dive—expecting to land in crunchy corn.

But noooo! Instead, he was sinking into a soft mucky goop that felt like it would swallow him up. He was thrashing around trying to grab whatever he could to pull himself out. He bumped into something solid and grabbed an edge. It was smooth and slippery! He couldn't hold on. "Help!" Hector called. "Help me quick!"

Ruby came through the hole which made everything dark again, but her voice called, "Can you find my hand?"

Hector waved his paw in the air until he touched Ruby's hand. She pulled hard and Hector came out of the goop with a weird sound of "thlurp!" Ruby backed up until he stuck his nose out the small hole. Hector was glad for the edges of the small hole, which wiped most of the muck off his fur.

Ruby looked him over as he came out of the hole. She took a handful of the brown goop. "Hm, I think this is chocolate pudding topped with gravy. Let's make the hole bigger so you can see what's really in there."

Hector stuck his nose in the bag again. He didn't see anything that looked nice and crisp like he was used to. He pulled his nose out. "It smells so awful in there," he said.

"Does it?" Ruby said. "I'm used to it, and I can usually find something. But we can leave." He followed her down the outside of the bag and squeezed through the trash bin hole at the bottom. This cleaned off more of the brown goop.

That night, as Hector tucked into bed, he thought over his day. "If I am going to live here, I have to learn to find nicer food. The city is very different than the farm. I can't climb corn stalks or get a quick sneak into a barn. I'll have to work on this."

He thought of his family now watching the stars and sang to himself, "Twinkle, twinkle …"

Hector's thoughts were interrupted by Bernard's voice, "It smells in here, Mama." This time, Hector knew it was a complaint. He knew it was about him.

CHAPTER 5

The next day, Hector noticed a change in everyone's attitude toward him. Even Ruby was not as kind. As they played outside, the others would talk, make a decision, and then run off. He wasn't told not to come, but he wasn't invited. "Wait for me. Wait for me," he called. But they didn't wait. He just followed from behind. Hector couldn't think of anything he had done, but he could hear Bernard's complaint even now: "I'm still hungry. Let's go find something to eat."

The next morning, Hector was finishing breakfast when Bernard, Tiffany, Ruby, and George squeezed out the door and disappeared. Hector looked out the door to follow, but he didn't see them at all. He stayed home for the morning with Mama Mouse, who was quite upset. When the others finally came back, Mama took them all out for a long talk.

Everyone was polite that evening, but not truly friendly. Hector went to bed feeling sad and worried. He missed his own family very much. Right now, they would be singing about God loving things small. Hector needed that song tonight. Once again, it was difficult to feel really loved.

CHAPTER 6

The next day, Bernard invited Hector out to play with them. "Good," thought Hector. "Maybe the past few days are over. Everyone has bad days."

"Come on, come on," said the mice. "Come play in our new playground." Hector followed them across the lawn and around a corner to a patio.

"Let's play Hide and Seek," Bernard said. "You be the seeker. You stay here in the middle and hide your eyes for a while. We'll call you in a little bit. Then come find us." Hector was glad to be included. He did as he was told. All was quiet as he waited to be told to come find the others.

Suddenly, a big cat shot out the door, flew down the stairs, and pounced on Hector. Hector felt the cat's sharp claws land on his back! It was awful! He squeezed from under the cat's paw, even while the cat's nails scratched the length of his back. He dove into a pile of leaves, panting for breath. His back was stinging badly. His heart was stinging even more by Bernard's pleased voice, "Well, it won't be crowded at home anymore."

"Alone again. No place to belong." Hector felt tiny tears in his eyes. He kept repeating that awful truth until he finally drifted into sleep.

It was hours later. All was calm. Hector lay very still, listening. "Did I hear something?" He twitched his special heart-shaped ear. Then he heard a gentle whisper, like a breath, "Hector, I love you. I know you hurt."

"This is strange," Hector thought. "I am nothing but a small mouse deep in a pile of leaves. Am I known? Am I known by name?" Hector crept out of the leaves and looked to the sky. There was no star yet, but quietly Hector whispered, "God, if that was you. Thank you." He was still for a very long time in the wonder of what he had heard. His heart felt glad.

Finally, Hector crawled to the edge of the patio, peering into the dusk to see if there was anything ahead that looked like food. "I think there is a tree ahead. Maybe there will be fruit and roots to sleep in." He slowly inched forward, his back hurting with every step.

The tree was an apple tree with a nice surprise near it! A strange, large flower bent over almost to the ground, looking like the sun going down. Yellow petals surrounded a center of black bits. He ran his hands over the rough surface, and a few bits fell out. He carefully crunched one open. Inside was something small, almost like a kernel of corn, and it tasted wonderful.

Hector finds a sunflower.

He pulled out another bit. The center of the flower was full of this feast! "All this, just for me! No more trash bags!" Hector crunched away until his tummy was full. He tucked himself under a tree root for the night and thought over this day. "Thank you, Great God. Thank you for loving things small. Thank you for this food. Thank you for my home under this root. You know where I am."

The sad and terrible morning seemed long ago.

CHAPTER 7

Every day, Hector stretched higher and higher in the center of the flower to reach more food. Every day he ran around the tree to use all his muscles. Day by day, he was getting bigger and stronger. He was healing and happy.

One day when he was relaxing in the sun, a shadow slowly crossed his body. Hector looked up to see a large black bird, circling above him, and coming closer. He quickly dashed under a nearby bush, but he didn't have time to curl his tail around his feet. The bird landed right next to him and began scratching in the dirt.

"What to do, what to do? Please don't peck my tail. Help, Great God." he whispered. "Please help me," He took a deep breath and let it out slowly to stop his racing heart. He was quite scared. The bird would not stop searching for him and scratching the dirt. Hector worked hard at keeping his tail stick straight.

To his side, Hector spotted something creeping across the lawn with low steps. "It's the cat that scratched my back! "The bird at my tail! The cat coming closer!" Hector's heart began pounding even faster.

The bird watched the cat and fearlessly hopped towards him.

Hector jumped when the bird hopped, and his tail jumped too. The bird spotted the 'straight stick' jump! He planted his claws on Hector's tail, holding it flat to the ground, and pecked it several times. Hector bit his lip to keep from squeaking the ouch he felt.

The cat watched the bird look down and let out a yowl that made Hector's fur stand on end. The cat's fur puffed out, and he looked huge. He charged the bird, growling a fierce warning to get out of "his" yard.

And that was that. The bird flew off.

Hector quickly wrapped his tail around his feet and let out a long sigh of relief. "The cat? The cat helped me? My enemy was my helper?"

Hector looked up to watch the cat come closer and sit exactly where the bird had been. "This is my yard," he seemed to say.

"Lick, lick, lick! Lick, lick, lick!" Hector watched and listened as the cat cleaned its paws. Next, the cat licked his side. "Lick, lick, lick! Lick, lick, lick. Clean, clean, clean."

"Go away! Please go away!" Hector wanted to scream.

"Lick, lick, lick," continued as the cat was now grooming his chest. "Lick, lick, lick. Lick, lick, lick," went on and on. Then, just inches from Hector, the cat stretched out for a warm nap in the sun.

CHAPTER 8

Hector was tired of being so still. He was bored, and he longed to run around. "This seems like forever!!! He pictured making himself bigger with his own fur puffed out and shouting a fierce 'Boo!' It would feel so good to be strong and tough in the face of his enemy!

"You know that's a dangerous thing to do," he told himself. He was quiet for a few moments, deciding what he could safely do. "I know. I'll stay quiet and make up new words to 'Twinkle, Twinkle, Little Star.'" He continued to keep his body still, but his mind was busy. Finally, he had the new words in his thoughts:

> "Licking cat, so very silly!
> Who will ever believe this story?
> 'A Mouse Is Saved by a Very Brave Cat!'
> If you can, try to believe that?
> Licking cat, so very silly!
> Please go away, it's getting chilly!"

Finally, as if the cat had heard his thoughts, he got up, arched his back for a good stretch, and returned to the house. Hector crawled out from under the plant and stretched too. He ran around the tree a few times to move every muscle.

His food flower now dragged on the ground. He looked hard to find a few bits to eat. He searched among the apples, but his hand only squished into a mushy one. Trash bin images flashed in his mind, and he shuddered all over, remembering its awfulness.

Hector had thanked God many times for his daily life for his food, his home, his healing. Today he added, "Thank you for sending help from the cat. I don't have my family, but Great God, you are helping me. Thank you for caring for me."

Twinkle, twinkle, little star. Thank you, God, for who you are. You love things great. You love things small …"

Hector stopped and sang that part again, "You love things small."

Then he whispered that part again. "You love things small!"

And then he shouted it, with his very loudest squeak, *"You love things small!"*

"Thank you, God!" Hector shouted. He knew his loudest mouse squeak was not very big, but he knew somehow God could still hear him. *"Thank you, God, for taking care of me day by day and protecting me and protecting me from the bird and the cat!"* Hector danced a little dance and spun in a circle. And he shouted again, *"Thank you, Great God!"*

Quietly he whispered, "Great God, you know it is time for me to leave here. Please help me find a new home. I need food, and I would like to be warm and maybe have someone love me again."

CHAPTER 9

Hector said goodbye to his tree and his food flower, pointed his tail to the patio and his nose straight ahead. As he left the yard and slipped through the darkness, he could see a building ahead made of large rocks. He liked the rough walls; it reminded him of the fields he loved. He followed the wall around corners until he came to a patio. It had been a long night, and Hector was glad to spot a crack between two of the rocks in the wall. He crawled in and fell asleep.

It was voices in front of him—low, high, loud, soft, boys, girls, laughing, talking—that woke him up. Hector had never been so close to people before. All he could see were legs and funny things of all shapes and sizes at the bottom of the legs. He stayed tucked inside the crack to watch and listen and decide his next move.

"Where am I?" Hector wondered. He was puzzling over the funny legs and the voices, when suddenly a loud "Bong, bong, bong" rang out from above. Hector was so startled, he bounced up and banged his head on the top of his hiding place.

"Come on! Time for church!" people called. And as the bell quieted down, so did the patio. Big people went one way, and children entered a door near him. Hector bolted from his hole through that door as it was closing. Once inside, he spotted a strip of inviting darkness at his level. In he ran. It was cool. It was dry. It was quiet. It was safe. He breathed a sigh of relief.

After a time, the children left, and Hector crawled out to see what being "inside" was like. The room was large, and everything under him was soft and warm. There was lots of room to run. And he did.

When he finally returned to his little, dark room, he followed his nose to a box with a nice smell. He chewed away a corner to find something crumbly and sweet and easy to nibble inside. "This will do for food!"

But as the rest of the day and that night and the next day and night passed and nothing happened and no one came, Hector worried that he was trapped inside, all alone and for a long time.

CHAPTER 10

Finally, the next morning, when he was sleeping in the corner of the little room, the outside door clicked open. He looked up with sleepy eyes. Suddenly, his dark little room was filled with light. "Oh my, my! I must clean this closet. And it smells in here, too," a voice spoke. "Now, where are the markers?"

Hector crawled from his corner to hide behind a large can on a shelf. He watched an older lady set up the room for lots of activities. She was singing a song and had a nice smile on her face.

"She looks like a kind lady. I wonder if she will like me."

When she was done setting up, she sat near a table with a big picture. It was a man looking into the eyes of a little boy holding a rock. Hector looked at the picture a long time and wished he was in the boy's hand and being looked at by such kind eyes. The lady's eyes were closed, but her lips kept moving. She ended with, "Thank you, Jesus. It's a good day to be a good day."

Just as she stood up, children came bursting through the doorway. The room was suddenly noisy. Hector stayed close to the can and wrapped his tail around his feet.

"Hi, Miss Annie. Look what I brought." Several children had small objects in their hand or a little box.

Miss Annie greeted each one with the same kind eyes as the man in the picture. "Oh, what a treasure," she said as she looked in their eyes.

"Was she talking about what they brought or about them?" Hector wondered.

From behind the can, Hector watched children building with magnetic blocks. Another group at a table were roughly outlining each other's hands. Two boys were playing a game on a small table between them.

Miss Annie was greeting two new visitors, "Welcome to morning class, Josie and Juniper. This is Jackson, Olivia, Lyla, and Maya. Over there, Carter and Dominic are building, and Samuel and Lucas are playing a game." Everyone stopped and said hello.

Today we are making leaves for a "Thanksgiving tree." Lyla can show you how to roughly trace your hands. So far, we have Thanksgiving leaves for our pets, families, friends, and favorite foods. Today, we've brought favorite small things from nature."

In group time, the children told what they liked about the little flowers, leaves, seashells, and bird's egg they brought in. "Aren't small things wonderful!" Miss Annie said.

Hector wanted to stand up and squeak out, "Hey, you've got a small mouse in your classroom. I think you would like me." But then he dropped back down. "Do inside people like mice? I'm not so sure."

"Lucas, you brought a very interesting rock today," Miss Annie said. "Tell us about it please." Lucas wheeled his chair to the front of the group.

"This is a piece of black quartz from my rock collection," Lucas began. "Quartz is the second most common mineral on earth and can be part of many other rocks. When it is in sand form, it helps make glass. I have quartz rocks in other colors—clear, milky white, pale pink. Quartz is used for kitchen countertops now. Big slabs of quartz are made in factories in a short time, but it takes a special high heat. When quartz is made on earth, it can take thousands of years to form and can be millions and even billions of years old. Quartz never changes once it forms."

"Thank you, Lucas. Any questions?"

"Was God alive a billion years ago when the quartz was made?" Samuel asked.

"I think He was alive and has been God a long, long time," Maya added.

The children added more leaves to the Thanksgiving tree and cut extra leaves. "This will be taken upstairs for church next Sunday. The tree will be up through Thanksgiving Day and the next Sunday," Miss Annie said. "Hopefully, it will be full, full, full of our thanks–givings."

Hector watched and listened and realized he was enjoying the children. They were noisy and busy and fun to watch. When they said "Good-bye" to Miss Annie, he was sorry to see them leave.

CHAPTER 11

Hector was becoming aware of a *big* problem in the closet. It had to do with pooping. He had made a very nice bed at the back of the closet by tearing up a roll of paper towels. He did not want to use his bed as a bathroom. He hadn't really solved this inside problem. Hector knew he was leaving telltale poops around the edge of the closet, and it was getting smelly. The next time Miss Annie came to set up the class, she closed the door. They all went outside for the day.

After the children left, a man came with Miss Annie and opened the closet door.

"Yup," he said. "Smells like a mouse, and it's not nice. They are such pests!"

Hector felt quite ashamed. This was not a problem when living outside. Now he had been found out. He wished he knew the way to fix it.

The man looked at Hector's food source. "These cookies have been eaten by a mouse for sure. I'll dispose of them for you." Just like that, his food source was gone. "This closet needs to be cleaned and sterilized. I'll do that tomorrow."

"For now, I can put pellets down that the mouse will like.

When they are eaten, the mouse will die, and I'll throw it away tomorrow."

"Oh, dear," said Miss Annie. "Could I put down a cage with some good food in it? Maybe the mouse will go in there, and we could have it as a classroom pet."

"You can cage this mouse, and the children could watch it but not touch it. Are you sure you want to do this? You'll have to wear gloves when you clean the cage."

"The children will enjoy it. Mice are fun to watch. I have a hamster cage at home," said Miss Annie. "Shall I put cheese in?"

"No cheese," replied the man. "Maybe a little peanut butter on a piece of celery or a few seeds, like sunflower seeds." He laughed. "I can't believe I'm helping you be nice to a mouse."

Miss Annie left. While she was gone, Hector realized he did not like being called "it"! I am Hector—a real mouse, a nice mouse. I am small, but I am known and loved by God. I am not a pest! I am not an "it"!

Hector hid in the back of the closet and watched the man put pellets down. They smelled good, but he knew not to eat them. Miss Annie returned with a cage, and Hector watched her set it up. She put newspaper on the floor and paper towels in a corner. She filled a shallow dish with water and sprinkled sunflower seeds in another corner. "That's what I ate from my food flower. I love those!" Hector watched Miss Annie prop open the door with a stick.

Well, little mouse," she said as she placed the cage on the floor of the closet. "I'm giving you a chance. I hope you take it." She shut the closet door.

Hector sat outside the cage, thinking. "My food is gone. I can't eat those pellets. This cage is clean. I like that wheel thing. Is this the answer? I might get bored being in such a small space, but I can watch the children. If I don't go in, what should I do? I've got to eat. Should I try to go back outside?"

Then he pictured the yucky trash can, the mean cat, and the fearsome bird. "It's a no. Maybe the children will love me as they watch me.

But what about my stars? It's already hard to remember the stars and my family singing. I would have to give up the stars. Is this right, Great God?"

Hector twitched his special, heart-shaped ear and waited. There was no voice. But this seemed like a good choice. "I asked Great God for a warm place and food and someone to love me. This answers all of that, even though it is not what I expected."

Hector carefully stepped into the cage and used his tail to knock the stick over. The door banged shut. "This is my new home. It's clean, it's nice. It has nice food." He ate a lot and then spent time ripping up the paper towels to make a soft bed for sleeping.

And that's how Miss Annie and the man found him the next day. "He looks healthy," the man said. "You can keep him as long as the children are willing to just watch and not touch him."

"Should I go in?"

CHAPTER 12

The next time class met, the children gathered around the cage to watch the mouse that had been rescued.

"Look at his funny ear."

"It's heart-shaped, isn't it? I wonder what the story is behind that ear." Miss Annie said. "Let's name this mouse."

"Dozer," said Jackson. "Our dog is named Dozer. I like that name."

"Valentine," said Olivia, "for his funny ear."

"Cutie Pie," Lyla offered.

"Is this a girl mouse or a boy mouse?" Dominic asked.

"I really don't know," said Miss Annie. "Let's have some boy names. And names that could go either way."

"Max! Chester! Superman!" Samuel called out.

"Cat," Carter added. Everyone knew Carter loved cats.

Calling a mouse "Cat" brought much laughter for everyone.

"Please don't call me 'Cat,'" he squeaked. The thought of being called "Cat" made him shudder.

Things got even sillier. "Let's name him Frog."

"How about Turtle?"

"How about Pineapple?" It's perfect." Maya explained. "He's

brown and rough on the outside. I bet he's a sweet mouse. Look at that face and his heart shaped ear."

"I'm not buying it," Dominic said.

Everyone was giggling. Hector ran to the side of the cage, squeaking loudly, "Hector. My name is Hector Mouse. I'm not a cat, a frog, a turtle, or a pineapple!" He was getting quite worried. He had always liked the name Hector.

Lucas watched for a bit. "I like the name Twinkle," he said. "He has eyes that shine a little—like twinkly stars. And it's not a girl's name or a boy's name."

Everyone stopped and looked closely to see what Lucas was seeing. Hector's soft brown eyes did have a small twinkle in them.

And that was that! His name was now "Twinkle" to the class and "Hector Twinkle Mouse" to himself. "I can live with that. I am happy to remind people of the stars I love." He did an especially fast run on his wheel to let everyone know that he was happy with his new name.

That night, as Hector climbed into his shredded paper towel bed, he thought about his day. "What I asked Great God for, He has kindly done for me. I have a warm home, nice food, and someone to love me. Thank you, Great God. You love things great, and you do love things small. And you love me. Thank you."

And Hector Twinkle Mouse went to sleep in his safe new home.

STORY 2

THE CHRISTMAS GIFT

Christmas Joy for Hector

CHAPTER 1

Hector was alone in his cage in an empty room. All was quiet—way too quiet. He missed the children who had left with "Happy Thanksgiving" and cheerful "Goodbye's" to each other.

Hector turned a slow circle in the middle of his cage, taking in every part of his surroundings:

> Clean bedding
> Hiding place under a little box
> Bottle of water
> Healthy food
> Wheel to run on
> Good-sized cage
> Safe place

"I have everything I need. I am thankful."

But Hector knew underneath those words, he was bored! "I'm bored! I'm lonely," he squeaked. "I've explored every inch of my cage. I can go very fast and very slow on my running wheel. I can find my food in the dark. I can close my eyes and find my water bottle!"

He thought of his family and the fields he used to run in. He thought of the scary parts of his life before his cage life: the ride from the fields in the back of a truck, the cat that scratched him deeply, and the kind voice he had heard in his heart-shaped ear, "Hector, I love you. I know you hurt." There was the terror of the big bird and the surprising rescue by the cat. "I'm not grateful for it, but I wasn't bored!"

He sat looking at the spaces between the bars of his cage. "Can I fit between those bars? What could I do once I'm out? He pictured himself being strong and skillful. "As I leave my cage, I want to fly through the air and do a fancy flip before I land. I want to run around the room all free and do three somersaults in a row. I will be magnificent!" He dreamily squeaked, "That's what I want to do."

He ate a large lunch, in case it would be a while before he made it back. With fresh courage, Hector turned his head sideways and pushed his nose through the bars; sure enough, his head, shoulders, and arms easily followed.

But right away there was a big problem! His full stomach bulged out on the other side of the bar and held him tightly in place. His back legs were kicking in the air. He was swimming sideways in mid-air and going nowhere! He was stuck!

He peeked down as best he could to hopefully spot a small table that held his cage! There was no table! "It must be smaller than my cage." The floor seemed miles away, and he was scared. "I can't go back. I can't grab anything. I can't drop to the table and fly from there!" He was quite dismayed.

"I just might have to wait for a very large poop."

He continued swimming in the air with his front feet and

kicking with his back for a very long time. Bit by bit his lunch shifted and what he hoped for finally followed. With great relief, he flopped forward enough to fall from the bars, clear to the ground. It was not the graceful flying through the air or the fancy flip he dreamed of. It was simply a "plop."

"Oh well! I'm out! I'm free! I can run and explore." He ran from corner to corner and along every wall. He ran from the corner to the middle of the room to do three somersaults. He tucked his head under in a hopeful roll forward. Instead, he skidded on his nose and came to a messy heap. "Not wonderful! Not what I hoped at all!" He took a deep breath and ran to the corner with the strip of darkness at floor level. He squeezed under the door to a clean smelling and very tidy space. "Oh, my. I don't want to leave any accidental telltale poops that I've been out. I need to get back to my cage."

As he was thinking about that, he heard footsteps coming down the walk.

CHAPTER 2

Hector squeezed back under the closet door and ran to the little table that held the cage. He reached up high to climb the table leg to his cage, but he slid back down. He tried again and failed; and tried again and failed again. The legs were shiny and slippery, with nothing to grip.

The footsteps were closer. Hector looked around and spotted the wooden door frame around the closet and the windows with narrow ledges along the bottom. He scurried up the closet door frame to the top, leapt from windowsill to windowsill and to the top of his cage. He squeezed through the bars and dropped to the floor as the door opened.

"Hello, Twinkle," Miss Annie called. "How are you today?"

He had almost forgotten his indoor name from the children. "I'm sure your food is getting low. Have you been well? Have you been good? Are you sleeping a lot?" Miss Annie chatted away.

Hector understood every word she said, but he was glad she didn't understand him, because he would have had to lie about being good and sleeping a lot. He didn't like that idea at all.

Miss Annie took down the last of the Thanksgiving decorations and taped a long, thick string of something bumpy from window to window. When she plugged the thick string into an electric outlet, little white lights twinkled above his cage.

"Stars up close! Stars up close!" He was so excited he jumped on his wheel for a quick spin. He squeezed into the corner of his cage and looked up as best he could.

"Thank you, Miss Annie," he chattered. "Oh, Great God, thank you for my indoor stars. You know I love them. Thank you for bringing the stars to me. I never thought I would see them again."

Miss Annie was smiling. "You seem to like these. Twinkly lights are a beautiful part of Christmas, aren't they Twinkle?"

"Christmas? What's Christmas? I don't know about Christmas. These lights are beautiful. I'm so glad the children are coming back soon. I've been so lonely. It's been too quiet. I've not been good really. I've run all over the room. I hope I didn't leave any poops." It all sounded like scratching and squeaking to Miss Annie, but Hector meant every word he said. He was very glad to tell her the truth.

CHAPTER 3

The next day, Miss Annie came and plugged in the twinkly lights right away. "Almost Merry Christmas, Twinkle," she said. "The children will be coming soon!"

It wasn't long before the door opened and children came to his cage, "Hi, Twinkle. It's good to see you!" Hector stretched up as high as he could and chattered away that he was glad to see them.

"I see Twinkly stars in your eyes today, Twinkle," Lyla smiled. "You must be happy."

At group time, Miss Annie announced, "Today, we'll be talking about this special time of year. What do we love about Christmas?"

Everyone called out a favorite part of Christmas: "Gifts! Surprises! Santa! Family! Singing! Lights! Christmas trees! Food!" Miss Annie wrote each one on a paper plate and put them in a circle on a bulletin board. The middle of the circle was empty.

"I wonder why we have so many ways of celebrating Christmas? There must be an important reason behind all of this. What do you think should go in the center?"

"Santa and presents are the best reason," Jackson said.

"I understand why you think this," Miss Annie answered. "The most important reason that goes in the middle is about a present. We can use the words 'present' or 'gift' to mean the same thing. Miss Annie pinned a picture of a gift box in the middle of the circle.

"I don't know if you still do this in school, but when I went to school, the teacher began every day by calling each name. When I answered, I would say, "Present." Then I asked myself, "Why am I calling myself a gift? I want you to know that each of you is a gift to me and to each other. You are present, or here, and you are a present."

"Jesus was also present and a present to the world. Here's how. Jesus and his father, God, were alike. When Jesus came, God was present with us in the world through Him. One Bible name for Jesus is 'Immanuel,' and it means 'God is with us.'"

"I wrote a poem about Christmas," Miss Annie added. "It is called

The Gift of Christmas

"God is with us!"
Oh, what a day!
Oh, what a way—
For God to show His love.

Miss Annie added a picture of Jesus in a manger to the gift box in the middle and her poem next to it. Jesus coming is the most important reason we celebrate Christmas.

"I brought a favorite rock today, "Lucas said. "May I share it?"

"Of course. We love your rocks and everything you know about each one."

Lucas rolled his wheelchair to the front. "This is what I call my Christmas rock. It's plain on the outside, but inside it has a surprise."

Lucas removed a slice of the smooth gray outside rock on top to show beautiful purple sparkling crystals inside. "It's called a geode. I think it is like Jesus. He was like all of us on the outside, but inside He was like God. He said and did wonderful things for people."

"It's super-cool," Carter said. "Did you find it?"

"My dad bought it for me as a birthday present."

"How did it get to be so pretty on the inside?" Olivia asked.

"This one could have once been a gas bubble in lava or maybe a fossil that died and left a space. But the crystals inside took millions of years to form."

"Thank you, Lucas," Annie nodded. "It's a very good picture of Jesus—plain on the outside and full of God on the inside."

CHAPTER 4

The next time the children met, Josie brought in a cage much like Hector's and placed it on a table near him. Hector stretched up high to see what was in the cage.

"We are leaving on a trip to visit my grandparents. Miss Annie said I could bring my hamster in for the class to take care of her while I'm gone. Her name is Tululu. I'm sure she will be a good friend to Twinkle."

Twinkle was happy to have a friend close by. He looked forward to talking together and getting to know her. He watched while Josie brought Tululu out of the cage and showed the class how to handle her gently. "You can touch Tululu because I bought her at a pet store. She's not like Twinkle. We don't know Twinkle's background, that's why we can't touch him. But my pet can be safely handled."

Josie put Tululu inside a clear ball that rolled around the room. All class time, the others made a big deal over watching her run inside a ball that pushed her around the room. It was funny when she bumped into the table legs and had to figure out what to do.

Hector watched her and the class. And watched. And watched.

He did his best trick: running up the side of his cage, swinging from the top, and landing on the floor of his cage. No one paid any attention.

"I feel invisible," Hector said. He squeaked as loudly as possible, "Hey, I'm over here. What about me? What about me?"

Class ended.

Tululu was back in her cage. She curled up in the far corner and went to sleep. Hector dropped down from watching her and crept to his far corner too. Tululu wasn't interested in being a friend.

CHAPTER 5

The next time the children met, Miss Annie brought out several tall figures made from a brown material. "Christmas is celebrated around the world, and I have several sets of figures that show the story of Jesus coming to earth. It is called a Nativity set. Each figure has an important part in the very first Christmas.

"These figures are from a country in Africa by the name of Uganda." Miss Annie showed them on a globe where it was in Africa. "A friend brought me this as a gift from there."

"This material that can become sticks or soft fiber is a dried leaf from a fruit tree that grows there. Any thoughts on what fruit tree that might be?

I don't think we can grow that fruit in our country."

After several guesses, Dominic finally suggested -"banana tree."

"Yes," said Miss Annie. "Isn't this amazing that a dried leaf could be made into all of these interesting figures?"

Ugandan Nativity Set

"This next Nativity set was an important part of my childhood, and I still enjoy setting it up." Miss Annie picked up several heavyweight paper pieces that fit together with a front, a back, and middle strips of scenery. "This is called a diorama. When I put it together and look in, I imagine I've crept up to look into the place where Jesus could have born. I'm not sure it looked like this, but I feel invited into this scene.

"Today, I brought shoeboxes, and I have various pictures to use to make your own Nativity set. Tip the boxes on their side, and cut up the lid to hold up pictures. I have pictures you can color, or you can draw your own. You may take your Nativity set home. Any other ideas for making your own Nativity sets?"

"I could draw one," Lyla answered.

"I have a clay that I can bake in the oven," Olivia offered. "I could make people and animals."

"I can build a set from Lego's," Samuel spoke up.

"Very good," Miss Annie said. "Bring them in if you would like to."

Everyone got to work on their shoebox Nativity sets, and Hector watched. He was thinking how he would have to leave his cage and get a closer look at all the interesting new things in class.

CHAPTER 6

That night, Hector squeezed through the bars of his cage and plopped to the ground. He knew the routine now—don't eat, drink a little water, use the bathroom part of his cage.

Hector climbed the wooden table leg to the paper Nativity set and spent a long-time looking in. He saw cows and donkeys, hay, a baby, a mother, and father. "I could easily have been there," Hector thought. "This doesn't seem very nice. It must have been hard for you to come from heaven to this kind of place. It's nice for mice. Why were you born in a place like this?" He didn't have an answer, but he continued to wonder about Jesus in the manger. "You left, and you came. You left, and you came. And it wasn't easy."

Hector left the Nativity set and headed back to go to sleep. He liked sleeping at night so he could be awake when the children were there.

Tululu had not. She was busy, busy, busy on her wheel, which was squeaking, squeaking, squeaking.

"Yikes! Doesn't she know that the children will come soon and she'll be rolling around for them?" Hector was quite grumpy about all the attention Tululu was getting. He had to admit—Tululu was "adorable." He had heard those words, "She's so adorable, so sweet, so soft, so ... so ..."

Meanwhile, he was just Hector, and it was, in fact, hard now to be called Twinkle. He wasn't smiling inside anymore, and he suspected his eyes didn't have 'happy stars' in them either. He felt increasingly invisible, and he was tired. Every night he had to put up with the squeaky wheel! Lately, he curled up to sleep, even when the children came. Loneliness had crept back into his life. Tululu did not seem friendly at all. She didn't need to be. She had all the attention of the class.

CHAPTER 7

The next night, when he had escaped his cage and sat in front of the Nativity set, he remembered again that Jesus left heaven and came to earth, and it was hard. "I haven't really left my safe cage and gone over to meet Tululu. I guess it is the Christmassy thing to do—to go meet her."

He looked at his usual path home—up the frame of the closet door, across the two windows, and a short jump to his cage. "I might be able to jump to Tululu's cage." Hector hurried to make the trip before he lost his courage. As he left the windowsill, he jumped higher and stretched further—and landed on the top of her cage.

Tululu looked up, surprised to see him so close.

"I haven't met you yet, so I've come to say hello," Hector spoke as he made his way to see her face to face. Did she even understand him? He suddenly wondered if they could understand each other, so he just repeated, "Hello."

She answered back in hamster chirps and squeaks, and Hector got some of the words. "Hi," she said. "Nice ... meet ..."

"I'm called Twinkle," Hector said. "My real name is Hector."

Hector makes a new friend.

Tululu nodded her head. "My ... Serena ..." And her eyes looked sad. " ... miss."

"Oh, I understand, I understand," Hector said. He was amazed they had this in common. "Do you like it here? Everyone likes you."

"No ... ball."

"You don't like the ball? It's fun to watch you. You get all the class attention."

"No ... scary ... bump ...!"

"Oh, I see," Hector said. "I had no idea you don't like it." They talked about what they liked about their cages, the food, and Miss Annie. Finally, Hector spoke, "I better go now, Serena. I need to get a little sleep before the children come in. I try to sleep now to be awake for them."

"... good ..." She nodded and turned toward her sleeping corner.

Hector jumped back to his cage and squeezed through the bars. He was tired and hungry, but so glad he had gone to meet Serena. All the things he thought were true about her were not real at all. Hector very much understood about missing family. He liked her real name, "Serena." He would call her that.

CHAPTER 8

Lyla brought a Nativity set from Israel. It was beautifully carved from olive wood, with careful details. "My grandparent's visited Israel and brought home this set. We keep it on our piano."

Dominic brought a plastic set for children. "We played with this when we were younger. We didn't have to worry about breaking it. My mother gives one like this as a Christmas present."

"It's wonderful to see so many different Nativity sets from around the world and for all ages. They're all so interesting."

That day, Lucas's father came with his guitar to teach the song *Feliz Navidad*. "This is a familiar song that is saying, 'Merry Christmas' in Spanish. We sing that line three times, and the last line is 'Prospero año y felicidad.' That line means 'I wish you a happy and prosperous new year.' However, a popular English version of the song is sung as, 'I wish you a Merry Christmas,' with the last line sung as, 'From the bottom of my heart.' Our family thumps on our heart as we sing that part. We'll learn it both ways, in Spanish and English."

As they ended singing, Lucas's father gave them a challenge. "When you go home, learn to say 'Merry Christmas' in a language that is important to your family. Christmas is celebrated around the world, so next week, we'll sing Merry Christmas in several languages."

Miss Annie finished with an exciting announcement. "We are learning a song in Spanish, because in two weeks we will celebrate a wonderful Latino tradition called *Las Posadas*. I know your family celebrates this, Lucas. Will you explain it to us, please?"

"*Las Posadas* means 'inns.' In Jesus's day, inns were homes that were open to visitors. For *Las Posadas*, we travel from door to door. The person acting as Joseph asks for a room for Mary, who is very near having her baby. At some doors, the innkeeper says, 'No,' and gives reasons why. But at the last door, the innkeeper gives them a place with the animals. That's where Jesus ended up being born. Then we all sing *Feliz Navidad* as we go in for Christmas lunch together."

Everyone left very excited for what was to come.

CHAPTER 9

Hector often went over at night to visit with Serena. They talked about their families and what they missed. Hector told her how much he liked the twinkly lights above their cages and how he thought of outdoor stars and his family singing together. He told her about the Twinkle song and sang it as best he could. He still remembered every word.

Then they serenaded each other with *Feliz Navidad*. "Let's sing it in our own language," Hector suggested. "I'll go first."

> Squeak, squeak—squeak, sq, squeak.
> Squeak, squeak—squeak, sq, squeak.
> Squeak, squeak—squeak, sq, squeak.
> Squeak, sq, squeak, sq, sq, squeak. (He thumped his heart.)

Serena's song had many more sounds:

> Squeak, squeak, Chirp, chirp, chirp.
> Squeak, squeak, Chirp, chirp, chirp.
> Squeak, squeak, Chirp, chirp, chirp.

Click, cl, Click, cl, cl, Click! (She patted her
heart.)

Another night, Serena touched her own ear and pointed to
his ear.

"My heart-shaped ear?"

She nodded.

"I caught it on a bush once and tore the end on a thorn. It
made this shape. My mama told me that hearts are for love, and
maybe I would hear words of love in my ear. That happened
twice."

He told her about how his mama had whispered in his ear.
Then he told her the whole long story of leaving the fields and
ending up in the city. He told her about how alone and frightened
and hurt he felt after the terrible morning of Bernard's meanness
and the cat's attack. "But while I was buried in a pile of leaves,
I heard a voice in my special ear say, 'I love you, Hector. I know
you hurt.' I think it might have been God."

"I ... no ... voice," she said.

Hector was quiet for a minute. The voice that breathed in his
special ear meant so much to him. "I thought everyone heard the
voice. I haven't heard the voice since. When I stop to really thank
God for as many things as I can, I feel His nearness. Sometimes,
I ask God for something, and when it happens, I say 'Thank you,
God.' He doesn't always answer, but when I do get an answer, it
helps me know He's heard my talking to Him."

"Maybe … " said Serena. Hector left Serena alone. He went to his favorite Nativity set, the paper one, and looked in. "Jesus, you came to earth to show God's love. Would you please help Serena know you love her?"

CHAPTER 10

"Merry Christmas," Miss Annie greeted Hector and Serena as she came in the next morning. "I've brought a treat for each of you." She pushed a slice of apple and a lettuce leaf through the bars of each cage. "I hope you enjoy these fresh foods. It's been a while."

Right away, Serena began munching on the lettuce leaf. She was eating very fast and enjoying it. Between mouthfuls, Hector could hear her saying, "Thank ... God. Love ..."

Hector ran to the side of his cage and began squeaking to her. "Did you ask God for this? Does this show you His love?"

"Yes ... asked." Her eyes were bright with happiness. And so was Hector's heart. It was a beginning.

That day, for sharing Samuel brought a Nativity set from Germany: It fit on the palm of his hand. A tree branch was carefully carved in half circles. The outer circle had a star. The next circle showed the animals. The smaller circle was Mary and Joseph, and the final little carving in the middle was Jesus in a manger. That part was the size of Samuel's fingernail.

Jackson brought a set of wooden figures that were all small.

There were lots of pieces—an angel, a donkey, shepherds, and sheep, Mary and Joseph, a tiny manger, and a little barn.

"Maya brought one that fit Mary, Joseph, Jesus, and a sheep in a tiny matchbox.

"These are all mouse and hamster-size nativity sets today," Miss Annie laughed.

Hector's ears perked up. "I must visit those tonight."

Lucas's father came with his guitar for Christmas singing. "I gave you a challenge to learn how to say 'Merry Christmas' in a language that is important to your family. Who wants to start?"

Carter spoke up first. "*Frohe Weihnachten* is German. My father is part German."

"Let's try it to the tune of *Feliz Navidad*." Lucas's father strummed for a minute. "It fits, doesn't it? *Fe - liz Nav - i - dad* and *Fro - he Welh - nach - ten* have the same beats. Shall we close with 'From the bottom of my heart?'"

"Sounds good," Carter said and added a thump over his heart as they sang the last line.

"I looked up *Merry Christmas* in Ugandan to go with my Nativity set,"

Miss Annie said. " It's *We - bal - e Kris - ma - si! Webali Krismasi, Webali Krismasi*—from the bottom of my heart." She moved the Christmas figures forward as they sang.

"Jackson and I are part Filipino," Olivia said. "So we would say, *Mali - ga - yang Pas - ko* in Tagalog. It has the same beats, but I like Spanish. Can we end with *Prospero año y Felicidad*?"

Miss Annie told more about the upcoming *Las Posadas*

celebration. "Come dressed as travelers from old, if you wish. The boys will take turns being Joseph, knocking at the doors, and pleading to be let in. Mary does wear a special dress with a pillow around her middle, so she looks pregnant. Maya, you're tall enough that you could handle the pillow around your waist. Would you like to be Mary?" Maya agreed.

"The innkeepers, your fathers and mothers, will be inside the doors," Miss Annie shared.

"I wish I could go," squeaked Hector.

"… me …," answered Serena.

In group time that day, they talked more about why Bethlehem was so crowded that year and how worried and anxious Joseph might have been as he looked for a place for them.

"Why didn't God make it all happen in a nicer way?" Maya asked.

"They seemed to be so alone, like God didn't care at all," Dominic added.

"It does appear that way," Miss Annie agreed. "We don't know all the reasons for the hardships. The next part of the Christmas story might have been one reason why it happened the way it did.

"We know Jesus came to bring God's love to all people on earth. "All people" means all kinds of people—important people and not so important, rich and poor, educated and not. Maybe to make that clear, God's angel went first to the shepherds in the open fields nearby. Shepherds took care of sheep all day and night in all kinds of weather. They slept outside and couldn't bathe often.   But they were the first people an angel went to with the announcement, 'Go find God's son, lying in a manger.' I think shepherds coming straight out of a field would have felt right at home in a place with animals and straw."

"I can picture that," Hector thought. "The shepherds and me, and any lambs they brought, would have all felt very much at home with the animals."

CHAPTER 11

The class was full of laughter and excitement that morning. It was the last time to be together before Christmas. Josie and Juniper had returned in time for *Las Posadas*. Hector watched them rush to Serena's cage and talk to her, "Oh, Tululu, we missed you so much. You'll be coming home with us today."

Hector sadly realized what would happen soon. He would be alone for a long time.

Everyone left the room to begin the *Las Posadas* journey to knock on all the doors of the church. Hector and Serena could hear Joseph pleading with the innkeepers to please take them in. The parents, pretending to be innkeepers, were having fun, too. They were either gruff and mean, accusing them of being robbers, or understanding but unable to help. Finally, they heard one say, "I have no room in my inn, but you may go with the animals."

Then the doors opened, and everyone happily sang *Feliz Navidad!* as they went in for lunch.

"Look at my dog with cow's ears on," Jackson said. "He's a very tiny cow!"

"Look at my new baby sister in the manger." Carter was happy to see her all wrapped up and looking at everyone.

When things quieted down, Serena and Hector talked about not seeing each other at Christmas.

"… miss …," Serena said.

"I will miss you, too, Serena," Hector said. "I'm glad we have become friends and all of our talks about God." It was hard to say goodbye.

"Yes. I'm glad we could learn about God together. Remember 'the Gift of Christmas: God is with us!'"

The children were whacking the piñata outside the windows. Suddenly a loud "crack!" sounded as they split the piñata open, and candy and gifts fell on the ground. The children grabbed handfuls of treats and then began trading with each other for favorites.

Las Posadas Fun

Soon after, Josie and Juniper came over to get Tululu's cage. Hector ran to the side of his cage to watch her go. "May Twinkle come home with us for Christmas, Mommy?" Juniper asked.

"Please, Daddy. Please." Josie added, "They're good friends."

"When we take care of Tululu, we'll take care of Twinkle. I promise," Juniper said. "We'll wear gloves when we feed them."

Their parents looked at each other. "All right. We'll give them a nice Christmas together," they agreed.

"Can we keep them in the family room, so they can see the lights on the tree? May we give them apple slices and treats?" Josie asked.

Hector looked at Serena with happy eyes as their cages were picked up. It was not going to be a long, lonely Christmas after all.

CHAPTER 12

Christmas was more than wonderful at Josie and Juniper's home. The lights on the tree stayed on for hours. Every time Hector looked at the tree, he felt happy. He and Serena enjoyed lots going on every day. The air filled with the smells of good things baking, cheerful music playing, and visitors dropping by. Serena usually came out of her cage to explore a visitor's hand. Hector knew he wouldn't be asked to do that, but now he didn't mind. Their cages stood close together, and they could visit at any time.

"Are you happy to be here?" he asked Serena.

"… home …," she replied happily. "Tululu … OK."

"Tululu it is," Hector replied.

On Christmas morning, Hector and Tululu were both given new silent exercise spinners.

"Yeah!" Everybody cheered, including a loud squeak from Hector.

Most wonderfully, little Christmas cakes appeared in their cages.

"How did you make those?" Daddy asked.

"You know how I love to cook, so I looked up how to make

treats for our little creature friends. These are made of dampened cardboard pressed into a cake shape and dried," Mama said. "They can gnaw away."

"We decorated each one with carrots and seeds," Josie added. "Juniper did this one, and I did Tululu's."

"I have another cake for us, too!" Mama announced. "I've baked a special cake for dessert today. Would you like to sing 'Happy Birthday' to Jesus?"

Hector was deeply happy all day. "This must be Christmas joy that everyone talks about. I see people loving each other in so many ways. I'm glad you came to earth, Jesus, to show us God's love," He whispered. "Merry Christmas to me and thank you to you."

Hector had a final little bedtime chew on his own perfect Christmas cake. He curled up in his sleeping corner with a happy heart.

He very much looked forward to a quiet night of sleep.

STORY 3

AN EASTER TO REMEMBER

Hector Solves a Problem

CHAPTER 1

Back in the classroom, Lyla and Olivia arrived with little boxes of various sizes for Hector's cage. He enjoyed climbing on something new. He usually ended at the box fastened up high where he could see more of what was going on in the room.

With Serena, the Christmas Nativity sets, and the twinkly lights all gone, Hector now nightly visited the large picture of Jesus that Miss Annie liked. The picture sat on a table and leaned against the wall. Hector could sit before it or curl up on the frame. He wasn't lonely when he did that.

In the picture, a boy held a rock in his hand, and was showing it to Jesus. Hector liked looking at Jesus' face. There was a little smile on his lips and his eyes were full of delight as he listened to the boy.

Night by night, the picture meant more and more to Hector. He pictured himself in the boy's hand and Jesus looking at him with love. He now came to look at the picture of Jesus and talk over his day – what he liked and what he was worried about. He asked Jesus to take care of his family and Serena. He chatted away in squeaks and bits and never worried that Jesus might not understand him.

CHAPTER 2

"Since we are between Christmas and Easter, we'll be acting out stories of Jesus' life," Miss Annie said. "Today's story is one of my favorites. Who has had the experience of not being able to see because someone was in front of you and blocking your view?" Everyone had either had that problem or helped someone smaller to see better.

"This is the story of Zacchaeus who was a short man. I sometimes wonder if he had been teased much of his life about being short, because he was not a kind adult. He worked for the government that had conquered his country. He was a "Chief Tax Collector" which meant the fearsome government could count on him to get all the taxes they wanted from the people. The heavy taxes meant people were very poor and life was hard. Zacchaeus even added another "tax" which was really money for himself. Zacchaeus became very rich, very lonely, and very hated.

One day, people heard the news that 'Jesus is coming to town.' By then, Jesus was famous, and people lined up along the road just to see him. Zacchaeus also wanted to see Jesus, but he couldn't. No one would move over for him to see. Finally, Zacchaeus gave up trying and climbed a tree. He happily watched Jesus come down the road.

Surprisingly, Jesus stopped right under the tree where he sat and called him by name. "'Zacchaeus, 'Come on down! I'd like to go to your house today!'

Zacchaeus did hurry down and off they went together, one tall and one small, while the crowd booed Jesus for talking to such a hated person.

'Zacchaeus must have felt great love from Jesus. 'I will give half of my money to the poor,' Zacchaeus told Jesus. 'I want to give back four times the money that I overcharged people on their taxes!'

Jesus looked at Zacchaeus with a smile. 'This is why I came,' he said. 'I want to help those that have lost their way from God to become my children again.'"

Hector watched the children act out the story. Samuel played Zacchaeus. He walked on his knees behind a wall of children and tried jumping up the best he could, but with no luck. A chair and a plant were on the table as a tree, and he climbed up to sit in the chair.

Dominic was playing Jesus. He chose to act as though the story happened yesterday. "Hey, Zach, why are you up that tree? Come on down. I'm hungry, and there's no McDonald's around. What's at your house for lunch? Let's go there." Off they walked together while the other children booed them.

The weeks went by, with reading and acting out more Bible

stories. Jesus healing a little girl, Jesus calming a storm, and Jesus feeding thousands of people with a little boy's lunch were favorites.

"You have true superpower, Jesus." Hector said one of his nights at the picture. "You have super love for people, and you make their lives better."

CHAPTER 3

Hector was thinking about an afternoon nap, when two visitors entered the room. He stretched up to watch.

"Hello, Pastor Dan, it's good to see you," Miss Annie said.

"Hello, Annie. I'd like you to meet Nyla. She is new to our church. She used to work in a bank and would like to help with our special project."

"Nyla, this is Miss Annie. She runs our morning class for the children and home schoolers." Nyla nodded a brief hello.

Hector looked Nyla over from top to bottom. She was tall, with brown hair in loose curls. She wore deep red lipstick, a blouse with a big print, a full skirt, and very high heels. She carried a straw purse over her arm. It was box-shaped, with an open top. It was big. All in all, she seemed to take up a lot of space in the room.

"As you know, you will be keeping records of the special offerings between now and Easter," Pastor Dan said. "The money will go to our local food bank." He placed a heavy, gray bag on the table. "Here are all the coins from our 'noisy offering' and the bills from the soup lunch last Sunday. I think there is a nice amount of money here."

Miss Annie pointed to a small chair. "Would you like to sit there?"

"I don't think so," Nyla said crisply. Hector could see it was a long way down for her to sit in a small chair, but he mostly didn't like her tone of voice. Pastor Dan apologized and went to find a bigger chair. Once he left, Nyla poured the bag with bills and coins onto the table. "You can do the coins, and I'll do the bills," Nyla instructed.

Annie picked through the coins and began sorting them into short stacks. She then slid the right amount into little brown paper rolls for the bank. It took all her attention to get it right.

Nyla swept the bills to her side of the table. Many were crumpled or folded, and she needed to smooth them out. From time to time, Nyla glanced at Annie. They were both busy.

Hector was curiously staring for a while, but suddenly blinked. "Did I just see that?" Hector wondered. "Did Nyla sweep a bill off the table?" Hector climbed to the little box that was tied up high in his cage where he could see her purse near her chair. It would be easy to brush something into that type of open purse. "It was so quick. Maybe I didn't really see that," Hector assured himself.

As they finished, Nyla filled out a form with the amounts they had counted. She put the sausage rolls with coins and the piles of dollar bills back in the bag. "Is Pastor Dan coming to pick this up, or should I take it to him?"

"He didn't tell us," Annie said.

"I'll take it to him, then."

"Thank you, Nyla."

"Yes," she said as she walked out the door.

"I don't like her," Hector said. "I wonder if she'll take even more money now. I don't know. I do know Nyla didn't say thank you or goodbye, and she left her chair for Annie to put away."

Miss Annie looked very tired today.

CHAPTER 4

One afternoon each week, Nyla came to count money. Hector always climbed to sit on the highest box where he could watch her carefully. Each time, while Annie was busy sorting coins, Nyla would flatten the bills with big motions and sweep one or two crumpled dollar bills from the table to her purse.

"How much has she taken?" Hector was angry. She was taking money that bought food for people that truly needed it.

That night, as Hector sat before the Jesus picture, he poured out his sadness and frustration. "I know it's not right! It's just not right!"

As he did, the story of Zacchaeus came to mind. "You helped him see he was wrong, and he gave the money back. Jesus, please help her do the same thing." Then he added, "Is there a way I can help? I only have one superpower. I can get out of my cage. I want to use my superpower for good like you use yours."

Hector stayed by the picture for a long time, until he had an idea.

CHAPTER 5

Easter was getting closer. Today the children were working on a garden scene to put out at church on Easter. Miss Annie brought in a large, flat, sturdy box, lined with a trash bag. They filled it with dirt and placed three crosses on a mound of dirt in a corner. "One of these crosses was for Jesus and the other two were for criminals," Miss Annie said.   She read the part in the children's Bible about Jesus dying on the cross, but they didn't act it out.

"See the shape of the cross. On this part that goes across, Jesus's arms were opened wide to the whole world. To me, it's another way Jesus showed his love. His arms are opened wide as if to say, 'Everyone, I'm doing this for you. I'll take the punishment for your sin, and you can be forgiven. It's my life for yours. Come back to God through me."

CHAPTER 6

That afternoon, Pastor Dan and Nyla came with the bag of money. "I can pick this up in an hour and head to the bank. It's our last collection."

"Now's my chance," Hector thought. He squeezed through the bars on the back of his cage and plopped to the floor. He followed the wall until he was behind Nyla. Her straw purse was close by her side. He ran quickly under her chair, up the side of the purse, and dropped inside.

Annie sorted change on her side of the table, and Nyla gathered the bills on her side. It wasn't long before two crumpled bills landed in the purse. Hector waited. The counting was done, and Pastor Dan arrived. "Thank you for your work. We didn't get quite as much money as I hoped, but it will all be helpful."

It was time for Hector to carry out his plan. He climbed out of Nyla's purse to balance on the handles. Hector braced for what he knew was next. Nyla was chatting away about shopping as she reached down to pick up her purse. Hector watched her fingers slip under the handle and closed his eyes while her hand came down on his own fuzzy body! Nyla began to scream and dropped the purse! Just like Hector hoped, the purse fell on its side.

What he hoped for, happened.

Pastor Dan leaned over to pick everything up. "What's this?" he asked. One crumpled bill lay on the inside edge of her purse and one on the floor. "Please explain this, Nyla," he said in a no-nonsense tone.

Nyla was quiet for a minute and then burst into tears. "Yes, it's true. I have been taking money from the offerings." She hung her head.

"Do you know how much you've taken?" Pastor Dan asked.

"It's been forty dollars every week," she said quietly.

"This is our sixth week. That's quite a bit of money. What were you going to do with it?"

"Celebrate my birthday," Nyla said sadly. "I was going to take myself out to dinner and shopping."

Pastor Dan looked at her a long time, "Do you still have the money?"

"Yes, I do. My birthday is after Easter. I haven't spent it."

He thought for a few minutes before he spoke firmly to her. "I need you to return all the money. I will write a report today that I want you to sign in case I need to contact the police over this. For now, it will stay between you and me. Return the money this afternoon and agree to do one more thing. I want you to work at the food bank for six mornings. You need to know these people and what this food means to them. I work at the food bank. I will know if you're there. Agreed?"

Nyla nodded her head.

"Let's go write up that agreement now. I'll go to the bank tomorrow."

"By the way, would you like to come to our house for dinner on your birthday? Annie, can you come?"

"I'd like that," Annie replied. "I make great cakes. What kind do you like?"

"Lemon cake, please," Nyla said gratefully. "It's a favorite of mine." Tears were still on her cheeks.

CHAPTER 7

Hector knew that the choice to leave his cage and end up on Nyla's purse handles might cost him his freedom. He was right!

Miss Annie wrapped a piece of wire mesh around the cage and over the top. The long bars now became tiny boxes. There was no escaping. He was trapped inside and quite sad.

When Josie and Juniper arrived for class, their mother looked at the cage and went to speak with Annie. "Over Easter vacation, our family is planning to visit a little farm in the country. I go there in the fall to pick fresh corn., but I hear they have strawberries now. I know Twinkle is a field mouse, and perhaps it is time to let him go free. What do you think?"

"That certainly sounds like the best for him," Miss Annie said. "Go ahead and take him with you today. Thank you so much."

The class finished the Easter-garden scene with rock paths and flower plants. They added a cave made from a small, dampened cardboard box, pressed into a lumpy shape. They used a round, flat rock that Lucas brought to put in front of the cave door.

"So, what is Easter about?" Miss Annie asked. "In this corner, we have the three crosses. What happened there?"

"Jesus died," Jackson added.

"We read about that in our children's Bible," Miss Annie said. "It's important to know and understand that part of Jesus's life."

"Once he died, his friends took his body off the cross and placed it in a cave. That's how many burials were handled then. A large heavy rock was rolled over the opening to seal it shut.

"A few days later, on Sunday morning, women friends of Jesus came back to visit the cave where Jesus was buried. To their great surprise, the heavy rock had been rolled to one side. When the women looked in, an angel said to them, 'Jesus isn't here. He is no longer dead. He's come back to life!'

"Jesus coming back to life is what we celebrate on Easter. This is important for many, many reasons. On that day, it was important because their friend, who had died, was now alive again. That Easter Day and in days ahead, Jesus came at many times to be with his friends and groups of people. People saw and touched his body, all healed and well. He was showing people that there is a wonderful life after death."

Miss Annie brought out a basket of colored eggs, each dyed red. "How many of you color Easter eggs?" she asked.

Everyone nodded.

"Easter eggs have been around hundreds of years. Because the new life of chicks come out of a shell, eggs remind us of the new life of Jesus. Years ago, the outside of the egg was only colored red. It reminded people of Jesus's death on the cross. The hard shell stood for the sealed tomb where Jesus was buried. The white egg inside, when the shell is cracked open, represents both the angel and Jesus's new life after death.

"People in many countries still celebrate Easter by this tradition. Each person has an egg, and as you crack your egg with another person's, one of you says, 'The Lord is risen!' And the other one answers, 'He is risen, indeed!' Try to crack your eggs gently. Hopefully you can do it three or four times. There's a chocolate egg for each of you when you're finished!" Miss Annie said.

Hector watched the fun with happy eyes as the children tapped their eggs and called out, "The Lord is Risen!' He is Risen indeed!"

"The Lord is risen."

"Happy Easter. I hope to see you Sunday!" Miss Annie added as she said goodbye to the children. Josie and Juniper picked up Twinkle and Tululu's cages. "And good-bye to you, dear Twinkle. We loved having you. May you find a nice home."

Twinkle stretched against the bars of his cage and began squeaking his heart to Miss Annie. "Thank you so much, Miss Annie. You saved my life. I am so grateful that I have been here. I learned much more than you know. Keep being wonderful to the children." He talked until the door banged shut, and then he was quiet. He felt quite sad.

CHAPTER 8

It was a beautiful spring day to be headed to a farm. Josie, Juniper, and their mom and dad drove along a smooth highway. "There's the barn," Josie called out excitedly.

After the turn, the road changed to a bumpy one. They parked the car and took Twinkle's cage to the edge of a freshly plowed field. Juniper set the cage on the ground, and Josie opened the door. Hector carefully stepped out. The dirt felt rough, but familiar on his feet. The sun was hot overhead, so Hector ran toward the coolness of the barn.

He didn't look back.

Josie and Juniper called after him, "Goodbye, Twinkle. Have a nice life."

Once inside the barn, Hector looked around. "Yes. This is my barn!" The cow was still chewing, chewing, chewing. The bags of grain along the side of the barn were as they had always been. He thought of the Christmas story as he slipped under a pile of hay.

Hours later, he woke up and could tell by the dim light that the sun had set. He left the barn and ran to the open fields and searched for the first star. He carefully circled until his heart-shaped ear picked up the sound of tiny, tinkly voices. He ran in that direction as fast as he could.

The words became clearer, "… thank you, God, for who you are."

He ran closer and could see his family all looking up. He picked out Mama singing, "You made things great, you made things small."

He was close enough now to hear Papa's voice with new words to the song, "You love things great, please love our Hector."

Hector stopped in front of them and looked up too. He joined in singing, "Twinkle, twinkle little star, thank you, God, for who …"

Everyone stopped singing and looked at him. "What? You're back!

Hector's back! I can't believe you are here!"

"Papa! Mama! Family! It's so good to be home. I have so much to tell you." They all began chattering news. And hugging each other.

"We have new cousins! We named one Hectorina after you."

"The farm is getting bigger. They planted strawberries."

Hector told about the day he was in a bag of corn and was carried away. "I will never go in a bag like that again. Let's all never do that!"

After a long time, Mama directed everyone to bed. Hector crowded into a favorite corner with his brothers and sisters giving him their warmth.

He thought over the long time he had been away. There had been hardship - but good too. "You were kind to me every day,

Jesus. You were always there to listen and help. You whispered your love to me when I was in the leaves. You led me to the food flower and rescued me from that bird. Miss Annie was kind like you Jesus. She gave me a chance to live."

He remembered visiting Jesus in the Nativity set and thinking how Jesus's place of birth was hard for him. "Then I did something hard. I got to know Serena. She was such a good friend." He thought of the long time he had talked with Jesus about Nyla's taking the money. "You gave me the courage to climb on her purse handles. It hurt when she squeezed me, but somehow you used it all for good. I'm home!"

Just like the picture of the boy and the rock. I am in your hand and your eyes are on me. I know that I am known and loved by you, Jesus. And that is the very best place to belong."

And Hector closed his eyes to sleep with a happy smile on his lips.

EPILOGUE

I hope you enjoyed this book and Hector's journey of a growing friendship with God. My journey in knowing Jesus includes an important memory. At my church was a picture of Jesus knocking on a door of a home. There was no handle on the outside for Jesus to open the door. It could only be opened from the inside. There is a story in the Bible that explains the door. Jesus is talking to us with these words, "If anyone hears my voice and opens the door, I will come into him and be his friend." *

When we ask Jesus to come into our lives, he come as a good and loyal friend. He loves us deeply. He has wisdom and help to guide us daily to be the best we can be. He may guide us to leave some things or try new things. He may help us stop bad habits and trade them for His better life. He promises to never leave us or walk away from us through the bad, good, or difficult times of life.

The cross is an important part of the Easter story. A friend of Jesus explained the cross this way: "Jesus carried the load of our sins in his own body when he died on the cross, so that we can be finished with sin and live a good life from now on. For his wounds have healed ours." *

I opened the door of my life to Jesus. I asked him to come into my life. "Please forgive me for anything I've done that makes you sad. Please guide me in my big and little choices so I live a good life. I want to be your friend too. Amen." Words like that is the beginning.

Talk to Jesus often as friend to friend. The Bible and other Christian friends are helpful. Bit by bit, God and you will begin to write your own wonderful story.

_____'s Place to Belong

(Your name)

is in Friendship with Jesus

From the Bible – Revelation 3:23 and I Peter 2:24 NLT

CPSIA information can be obtained
at www.ICGtesting.com
Printed in the USA
LVHW011303201122
733499LV00009B/648